TONIO'S CAT

TONIO'S CAT

Mary Calhoun
Illustrated by Edward Martinez

MORROW JUNIOR BOOKS
NEW YORK

Oil on canvas was used for the full-color illustrations.
The text type is 16-point Galliard.

Text copyright © 1996 by Mary Calhoun
Illustrations copyright © 1996 by Edward Martinez

Printed in Hong Kong by South China Printing Company (1988) Ltd.

1   2   3   4   5   6   7   8   9   10

Library of Congress Cataloging-in-Publication Data
Calhoun, Mary.
Tonio's cat / Mary Calhoun; illustrated by Edward Martinez.
p. cm.
Summary: Toughy, a cat, begins to fill the emptiness that Tonio feels
because he had to leave his dog in Mexico. Includes bilingual conversation.
ISBN 0-688-13314-2 (trade)—ISBN 0-688-13315-0 (library)
1. Mexicans—California—Juvenile fiction. [1. Mexicans—California—Fiction.
2. Cats—Fiction. 3. Pets—Fiction.] I. Martinez, Edward, ill. II. Title.
PZ7.C1278To 1996 [E]—dc20 95-35386 CIP AC

*To Michelle, to the St. Clement's breakfast workers,
and to the children of Las Palmas School
—M.C.*

*To my son Oliver and his cat
—E.M.*

What Tonio wanted most was his dog. But Cazador was
back in Mexico.

    What he wanted next was to play with the boys running
around in the school yard. But he was too new to join in.
He watched two of them.

That morning he had sat near those boys while they all ate sausages in the church hall across the street. Because many parents left for work very early, the church offered a breakfast program. One of the boys had looked at him and said something that made the other one laugh.

Something jumped out of a garbage can near him! It was a yellow-striped cat. A skinny old cat with a torn ear and a hind-leg limp.

The cat sniffed a candy wrapper. A stray. Hungry.

In Tonio's pocket was a piece of sausage from breakfast. He held it out. "Gato." Cat. He didn't know much English. But—he laughed—neither did the cat. "Gato, gato," he coaxed.

The cat looked toward the sound of his voice. The words were throaty, like a purr, not the clicking of *kitty-kitty*.

"Tienes hambre?" Are you hungry?

In Mexico Cazador licked food from his hand with a soft tongue. The cat snatched the meat so quickly, a tooth nicked his finger. Then the cat limped away.

In Mexico Tonio had told his dog good-bye. "No tengas miedo. Yo regreso pronto." Do not be afraid. I'll be back soon. He had pressed his face against the furry brown head, and Cazador had licked his tears.

Pronto? No pronto. Papá had a good job with a gardening crew. They would stay in California.

    Mamá had a job, too, helping an old lady. After school
Tonio walked alone, down and then up the curving street
to La Señora's place. It was on a bluff above the ocean.
Between the apartment buildings was a grassy hillside.
    Tonio sat there with the sea spread out beneath
him. In Mexico he had never seen the ocean. He
watched the waves coming, always coming, white

water swelling on the sand below. Sea gulls flew by.

In the long grass on the hill he saw something yellow. It was that same stray cat, crouched, hunting. Grass moved—a mouse. With a stick Tonio scooted it toward the cat, who pounced.

"Muy bien, gato!" Very good.

The cat looked up at him and went on eating.

Tonio's little sister ran out of the apartment ahead of Mamá. "Vámonos, Tonio!" Let's go!

He took Josefina María's hand. "Vámonos, gato!"

The cat flicked his good ear and turned his back.

Yet when Tonio looked...the cat was coming.

As soon as he turned, the cat veered off.

Another look, and the cat was following—no, leaving.

Each time Tonio turned around, the cat did, too.

He showed his sister. "Señor Gato is playing a game!"

They laughed.

At the steps to their apartment Tonio pointed to the hungry old cat. "Mamá por favor…?" Please?

She shook her head. No pets were allowed where they lived.

That night after they ate, Tonio asked Mamá for a
tostada. "Para el gato," he said.

Mamá laughed. Her tostada for the cat?

Papá understood. He told Mamá, "Tonio misses
Cazador."

So she spooned beans on a tostada, and Tonio put it
under a pink-flowered bush.

Tonio didn't see the cat, but in the morning the food was gone.

He put out scraps on Saturday and Sunday. Something ate them. Once he saw a yellow-striped tail disappear around a corner.

Monday in the church hall, one of the ladies who helped serve the breakfasts greeted him. "Hola, Tonio, hello!" said Guadalupe as she handed a plate across the counter. "Cheese pizza, and eat your peaches!" Tonio thought she was beautiful with her joking smile.

After Tonio ate and left through the patio, he saw yellow under a bush. The cat had followed him there! Tonio went back to the counter, and Guadalupe gave him a small piece of cheese pizza.

When he went to the bush, the cat didn't run. His yellow eyes watched Tonio as the boy put down the food.

"Te gusta pan con queso?" Do you like cheese bread?

Yes, any food. Tonio knelt while the cat ate. Then the cat butted his big head against Tonio's leg and made a rattling sound. A purr.

Pok! An empty milk carton hit the ground by them. It was thrown by one of the boys he'd watched in the school yard, José. His friend Guillermo started to pitch another carton.

"No!" Tonio jumped in front of the cat.

The cat didn't run. He bushed up to twice his size. *"Snaa!"* he hissed.

The boys laughed to see the brave cat standing his ground.

"Eres muy macho, Señor Gato!" Tonio exclaimed. "Se llama Macho."

"No, in English his name is Toughy," Guillermo told him.

Toughy went back under the bush to lick down his fur.

José grinned, jerking his head toward school. "Vámonos."

Tonio ran across the street with the boys.

And then the cat wasn't there. Not on Tonio's steps, not at the church, not in the school yard. One day, two days.

Each day after school Tonio went to the hill above the surging sea. No yellow in the grass, no hunting cat.

He looked at the wide ocean. His chest felt squeezed small.

As he walked the sidewalk near his apartment he saw two
little kids poking sticks into a cage at something yellow. It
was Toughy!

"Stop!" He rushed at them. "He's my cat!"

The boy stopped poking. "Sorry," he said. "We didn't know."

The girl said, "We were pretending he was a tiger." She opened the cage.

Toughy crouched inside, snarling and hissing.

Tonio squatted and said in a quiet voice, "Toughy. Cálmate." Calm down.

Toughy let Tonio pull him out and carry him. But when he struggled in Tonio's arms and the boy put him down, Toughy ran away. Angry old cat.

That night Tonio put out food. "Toughy? Gato?" he called and called. In the morning the food was still there.

Then, as Tonio walked, he saw the cat. Toughy followed, not closely, the way his dog had, but when Tonio got to the church, Toughy was there.

José and Guillermo came running. The cat arched his back and spat at them. They laughed. "Hola, Toughy!"

They sat with Tonio at one of the long tables. Breakfast that day was tacos. "Save some for Tonio's cat," said José. Guadalupe saw the cat out on the patio.

She poured milk in a bowl and took it to the door.
"Leche. Milk for Tonio's cat. We need a church cat
to catch the mice."

But at home that night when Tonio brought out food, Toughy was there. After the cat ate, he sat on the steps by Tonio and purred.

"Gato, gato," Tonio purred back.